M000006940

First Printing, 2022

ISBN-978-0-9975092-7-4
Email- corey@coreycarolina.com
Rise and Develop, LLC

Quarters, Nickels, and Dimes Oh My

Dedication:

This book is dedicated to my amazing children and my wonderful wife. Without them, my life would be meaningless. They have kept me focused on succeeding and providing a future for our family. Our family has been faced with immense challenges but the smiling faces of our children, have made every day a better day. My hope is that my children will inspire nations and keep their focus on doing their part to make this world better.